DISNEY · PIXAR

TOY STORY 2

Illustrated by Ben Butcher
Adapted by Christopher Nicholas

 A GOLDEN BOOK · NEW YORK

Library of Congress Control Number: 2005928189

ISBN: 0–7364–2394–X

www.goldenbooks.com

www.randomhouse.com/kids/disney

Printed in the United States of America   20 19 18 17 16 15 14 13

Do **you** like toys?

Well, Andy sure does. He has all different kinds of toys, and he loves to play with each and every one of them.

But Andy's favorite toys are a cowboy
named Woody . . .

. . . and a space ranger named Buzz Lightyear!

One day, something terrible happened.

Woody was **toynapped**!

You see, Woody wasn't just a toy.
He was a **FAMOUS** toy who once
had his own TV show.

Along with Jessie the cowgirl, Bullseye the
horse, and Stinky Pete the prospector, Woody
starred in *Woody's Roundup*.

Because Woody and the other *Roundup* toys were so famous, Al, a greedy toy store owner, was going to sell them to a museum—all the way across the world in **Japan**!

Jessie, Bullseye, and the Prospector were very excited. They had been in **STORAGE** for a long time.

But Woody didn't want to go to a silly **museum**! He wanted to go back home to Andy!

That is, he did until Jessie told him a story.
Just as Woody had Andy, Jessie once had a little girl who loved her.

They played together.

They laughed together.

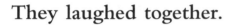

They spent every day together—until the girl grew up and forgot all about Jessie.

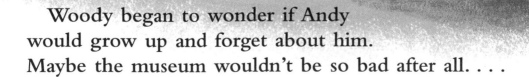

Woody began to wonder if Andy would grow up and forget about him. Maybe the museum wouldn't be so bad after all. . . .

Meanwhile, Buzz Lightyear had been
busy planning a rescue mission.

Mr. Potato Head,

Slinky Dog,

Hamm,

Buzz,

and **Rex**

all set off together
to find Woody.

To get to Al's Toy Barn, the toys had to cross a busy street. Fortunately, they had a plan.

Success!

Inside the store, Buzz and the others had to face another challenge—a new (and confused) Buzz Lightyear toy.

And little did they know that an evil toy named Emperor Zurg was hot on their trail!

But **nothing** would stop Buzz and his friends from finding Woody!

They quickly found Al in the office of the toy store and followed him to his apartment— and there was Woody!

But there was one **problem**.

Woody had decided to go to the museum with the other *Roundup* toys. He didn't want to end up **forgotten** and in **storage**.

Buzz tried to convince Woody to go home to Andy, but the cowboy had made up his mind. So Buzz and the others left—without Woody.

It didn't take Woody
long to realize that he had
made a mistake. His true
place was with Andy,
not in a museum!

But the Prospector had a different plan. He
was going to the museum, and no **cowboy**
would stand in his way. He trapped Woody,
Jessie, and Bullseye in the apartment. Then Al
took them away.

Woody's friends had to rescue him, but first they had to defeat **Zurg**!

Now they had to hurry—Al was on his way to the airport. Next stop, **Japan**!

Buzz Lightyear to the **rescue**!
Buzz, Mr. Potato Head, Hamm,
Rex, and Slinky borrowed a car
and raced to the airport.

They rescued Woody
and Bullseye—
and sent the
Prospector packing!

Unfortunately,
poor Jessie got
stuck on the plane!

Would Woody and Buzz be able to save her?

Of course they would!

Yee-haa!

Soon Woody, Buzz, Rex, Hamm, Mr. Potato
Head, and Slinky were back in Andy's room—
along with their new friends, Jessie and Bullseye!

All the toys knew they couldn't stop Andy
from growing up—but they wouldn't miss it
for the world!